A Snowman Enterprises and Lupus Films Production for Channel 4
Produced by John Coates, Camilla Deakin and Ruth Fielding

PUFFIN BOOKS

UK | USA | Canada | Ireland | Australia
India | New Zealand | South Africa

Puffin Books is part of the Penguin Random House group of companies
whose addresses can be found at global.penguinrandomhouse.com.

www.penguin.co.uk www.puffin.co.uk www.ladybird.co.uk

First published as an electronic edition 2012
This edition published 2020
006

Printed in China

The authorized representative in the EEA is Penguin Random House Ireland,
Morrison Chambers, 32 Nassau Street, Dublin D02 YH68

A CIP catalogue record for this book is available from the British Library

ISBN: 978-0-241-49156-0

All correspondence to:
Puffin Books, Penguin Random House Children's
One Embassy Gardens, 8 Viaduct Gardens, London SW11 7BW

"Come on," called Billy to his old dog.
"We're here! Let's explore our new home."

But Billy's dog was too old and
tired for exploring. As the months
passed he became slower and
slower, and then one day he died.

Together Billy and his mum
buried him in the garden.

Winter came. Billy was lonely.
He missed his old friend.

He had written a letter to Father
Christmas and was about to take
it downstairs when he tripped
over a loose floorboard . . .

"What's this?" thought Billy as he pulled out an old
shoebox. Inside he found a worn-out hat, some pieces
of coal, a shrivelled tangerine and a tatty green scarf.

As Billy unfolded the scarf, an old photograph dropped out. How odd! And then he realized. Another boy had lived here and made an amazing snowman.

"I'm going to make a snowman too," thought Billy. "Just like his one!"

He took the box
and ran outside,

and began to build
his *own* snowman.

He used two pieces of coal for the eyes and
a new tangerine for the nose . . .

and, last of all, he gave him a great big smile.
His Snowman was perfect.

But there was still
plenty of snow left.

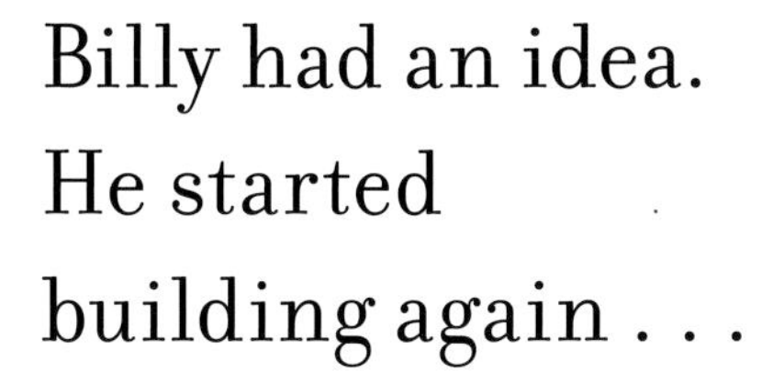

Billy had an idea.
He started
building again . . .

and bit by bit, with two socks for ears, he made . . .

. . . a Snowdog!

Now it was late. Billy said goodnight
to his two new friends and went inside to bed.

At midnight, Billy was
woken by a muffled bark.

He peered out of the window and rubbed his eyes
in disbelief. Did the Snowdog move?

He ran downstairs and
flung open the back door.

And then the most magical
thing happened!

The Snowman and the Snowdog came to life!

The Snowman politely shook his hand, and the Snowdog bounded up to say hello.

Then he was off up the garden where he found the old dog's ball. He wanted to play!

But the Snowman had found something too. It was a sledge.

Billy climbed on board. Out through the gate they went, towards the park and up the hill.

When they reached the top, Billy gasped in amazement.

The air was full of flying snowmen, rising up from the gardens below. What a magical sight!

Suddenly the Snowman took Billy's hand and started to run.
Billy grabbed the Snowdog and before he knew it . . .

. . . they were **flying!**

Low over the rooftops they flew,

then high above the city

and out across the countryside . . .

All of a sudden the Snowman sneezed and his tangerine nose blew off.

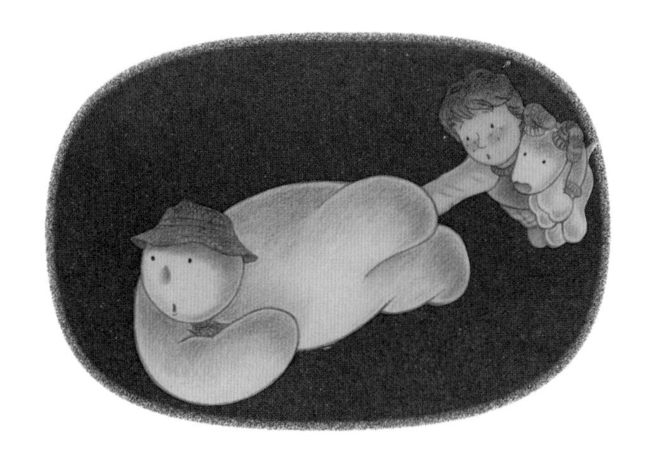

They swooped down to find it, but when they landed they found something really exciting.

"Oh!" cried Billy. "An aeroplane!"

Together they went to take a closer look.

They climbed in and, with
the Snowman at the controls,
they were flying again.

Out to sea they flew, on and on
towards the North Pole . . .

And what a sight greeted them when they arrived.

There were snowmen an

They had all come

nowwomen **everywhere!**

to compete in *The Snowman's Annual Downhill Race*!

Billy and the Snowman reached the starting line just in time. The whistle blew and they were off!

Twisting and turning, they sped down the course. Soon Billy and the Snowdog were the only ones left, battling it out with a penguin.

And, just as it seemed certain the penguin would win, the little Snowdog stretched forward and broke the finishing-line tape with his nose.

They had
WON!

Amidst the celebrations,
Father Christmas arrived.
He handed Billy a small
parcel. "This is for you.
Happy Christmas!"

But there was no time to open the parcel . . .
Dawn was breaking and it was time to go.

When they landed in Billy's back garden
it was time for him to go back inside to bed.

"I wish you could come with me," said Billy, "but you would melt indoors." Billy's eyes filled with tears.

He reached into his pocket for a hankie and instead found the present from Father Christmas.

Quickly he unwrapped it. Inside was a brand-new dog collar! He fastened it around the Snowdog's neck.

"There you are," he said. "Just like a proper dog!"

He turned to go, but as he did so the Snowdog's collar started to glow, brighter and brighter until suddenly . . .

"Woof!"
And where the Snowdog had been was a real live dog, his tail wagging with delight!

"Oh!" cried Billy, scooping him up. "You're just what I asked for in my letter to Father Christmas!"

Overjoyed, he hugged the Snowman, and then it was time to go inside.

Back in his bedroom, Billy waved goodnight to the Snowman.

Then he snuggled down in bed with his new friend.

"I think I'll call you Socks," he said, as he drifted off to sleep.

But when Billy woke up, Socks was nowhere to be seen. Billy's heart sank. Had it all been just a dream?

Then, hearing an excited bark, Billy rushed downstairs.
And there was Socks, waiting to go outside and play.

Billy opened the door and out Socks sped,
bounding towards the Snowman . . .

But the Snowman was gone,
melted away in the early morning sun.